Rudy and the Owl

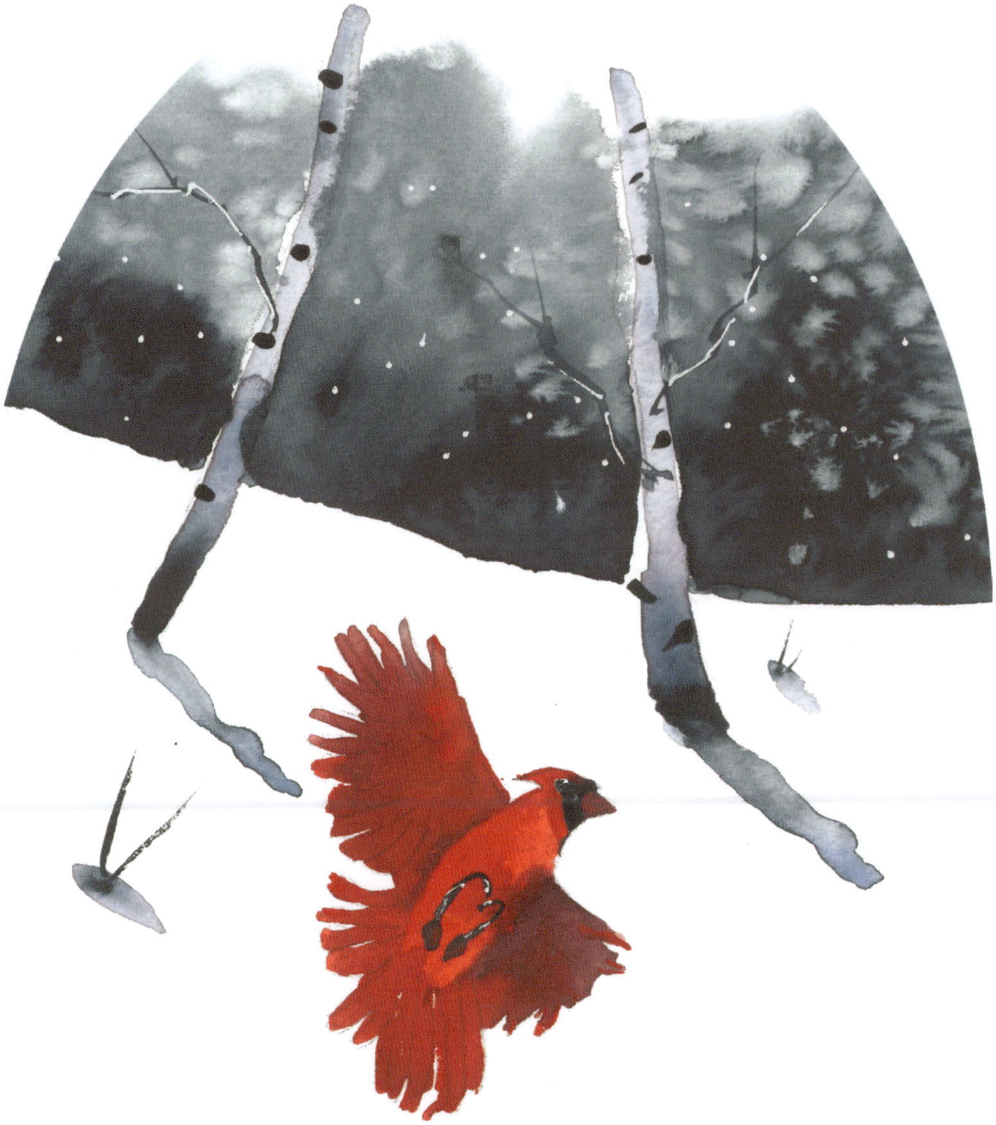

Rudy and the Owl

by Dolores Frazer

illustrated by Jim Lagasse

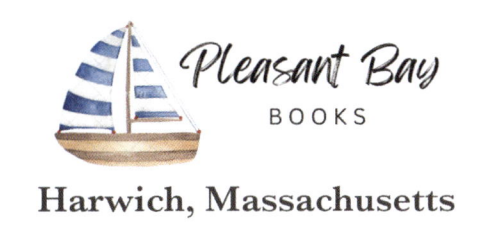

Pleasant Bay
BOOKS

Harwich, Massachusetts

Copyright © 2023 by Dolores Frazer

All rights reserved.
No part of this book may be reproduced or
used in any manner without written permission
of the copyright owner.

First edition October 2023

Illustrations by Jim Lagasse

ISBN 979-8-9886695-0-0 (Hardcover)
ISBN 979-8-9886695-1-7 (Paperback)
ISBN 979-8-9886695-2-4 (eBook)

Library of Congress Contol Number 2023913553

Published by Pleasant Bay Books
Harwich, Massachusetts
pleasantbaybooks@gmail.com

www.doloresfrazer.com

*To my grandsons
Henry, Grant, and Leo*

*May you hear our call
and find us.*

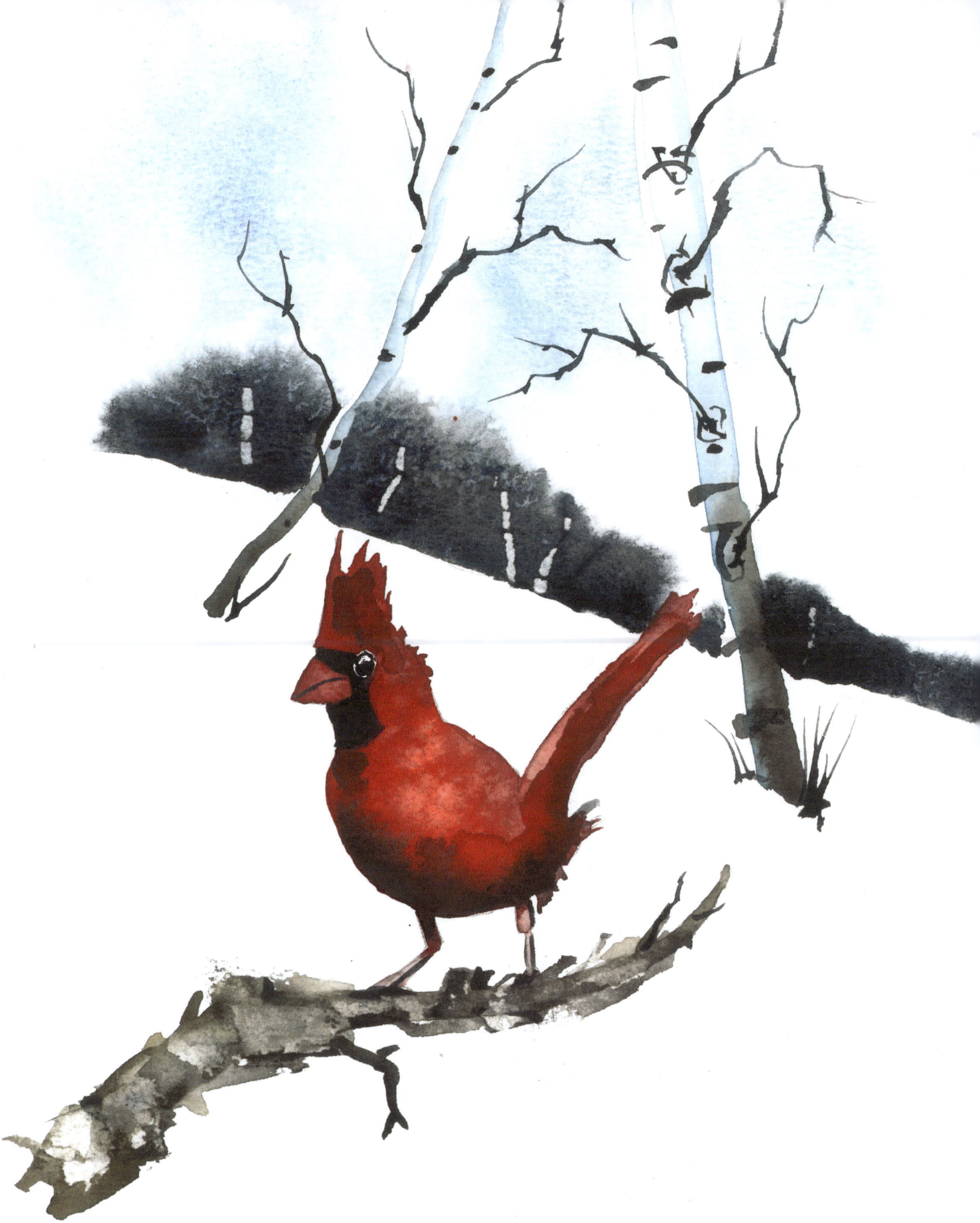

Rudy adored when hoots filled the night sky.
He wondered who made that sweet sound, and then why.

The moon, from up high, had a marvelous view.
So one night Rudy asked it, "Who makes that *hoo-hoo*?"

The moon responded to Rudy's delight.
"It is the owl's hoots that you hear each night.
His strong wings and sharp sight give the owl his might,
but he stars in the show when he *hoo-hoos* at night."

Rudy was thrilled and had to find out more.
This was a chance that he had to explore.

"Wouldn't the owl and I make such a good team?
To sing with an owl would be living a dream."

"How can I find the owl whose hoots I hear?
I'm little, but strong, and can search far and near."

Rudy's high spirits were hard to resist.
The moon could help, and she was glad to assist.

"When I am full and round, and shine real bright,
be ready to travel some distance in flight."

Rudy knew he could make his dream come true.
He'd meet the owl, and he'd sing with him too.

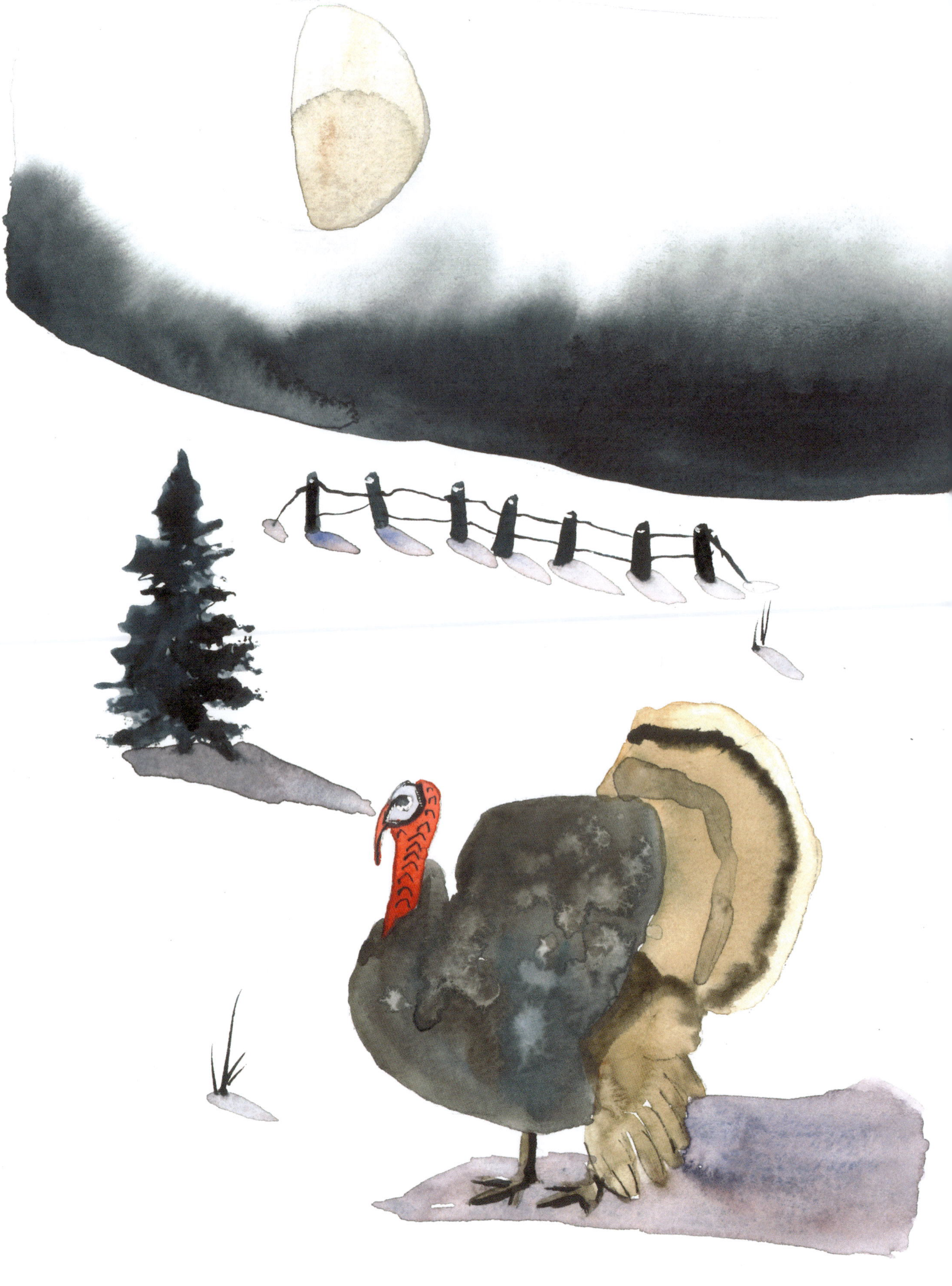

A few days later, the time seemed so right.
A half moon appeared just before it was night.
Maybe the moon did not need to be bright.
The late day sun still gave plenty of light.

So Rudy awaited the owl's fine *hoo-hoo-hoo*
'til he heard a soft gobble, a sound that was new.
He flew down to look, and that's when he spied—
a remarkable bird with a confident stride.

Rudy was puzzled, so he asked the bird why he chose to walk when he had wings to fly.

"Turkeys prefer to have feet on the ground. It is quite hard to fly with a body this round."

"Speed is my challenge since I am so small. To meet an owl, I must follow his call."

"Even up close, the owl is hard to see.
His feathers are marked so they blend with the tree."

One dark starlit night with no moon in view,
Rudy awoke to the owl's *hoo-hoo-hoo*.
"It must be a dream," he thought, "but if it's not,
an owl is nearby where he's easy to spot."

At first it was just a faint shadow he spied—
an upside down bird with his wings spread out wide.
"Is that the owl I see hanging near my nest?
Were those his hoots that woke me from my rest?"

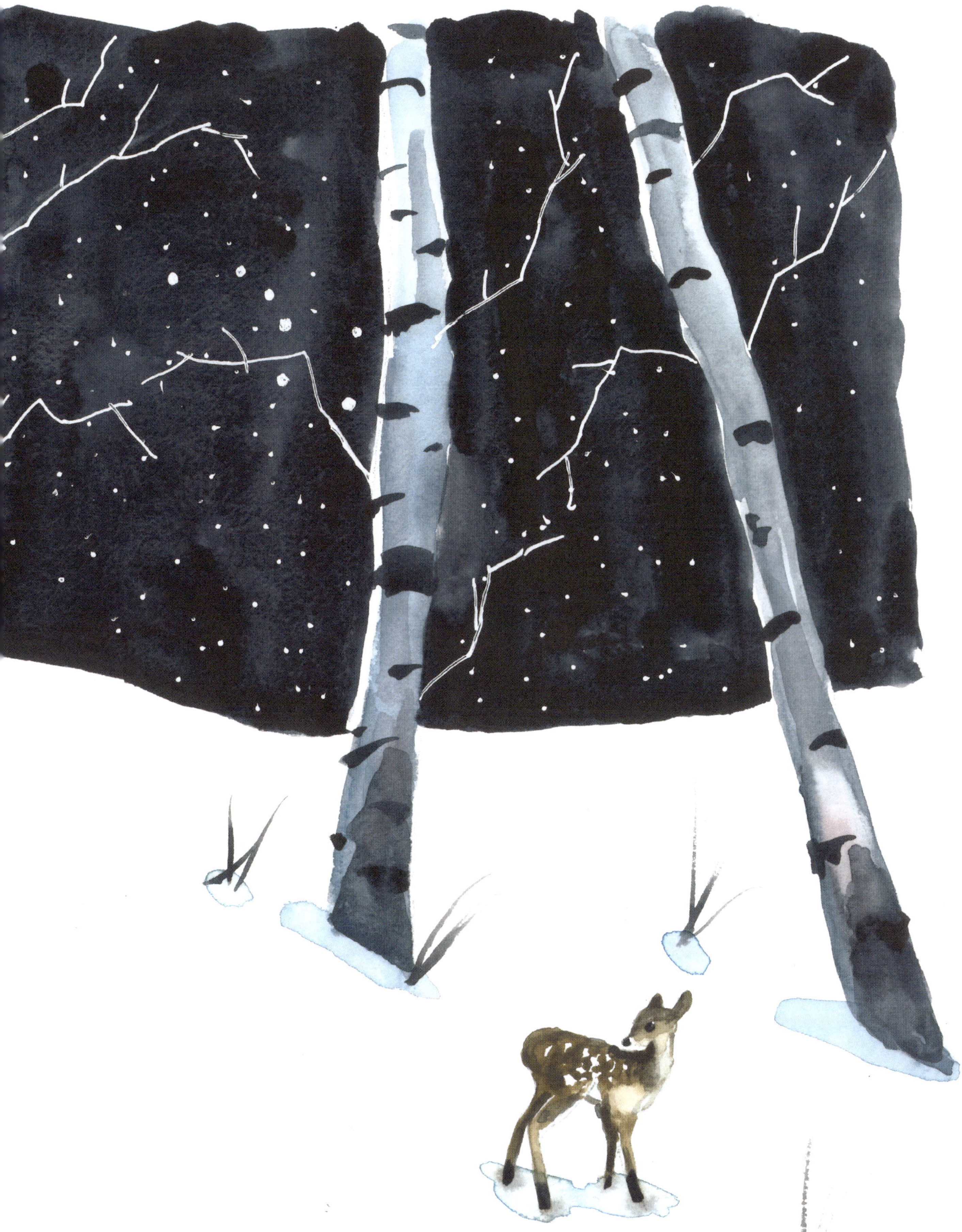

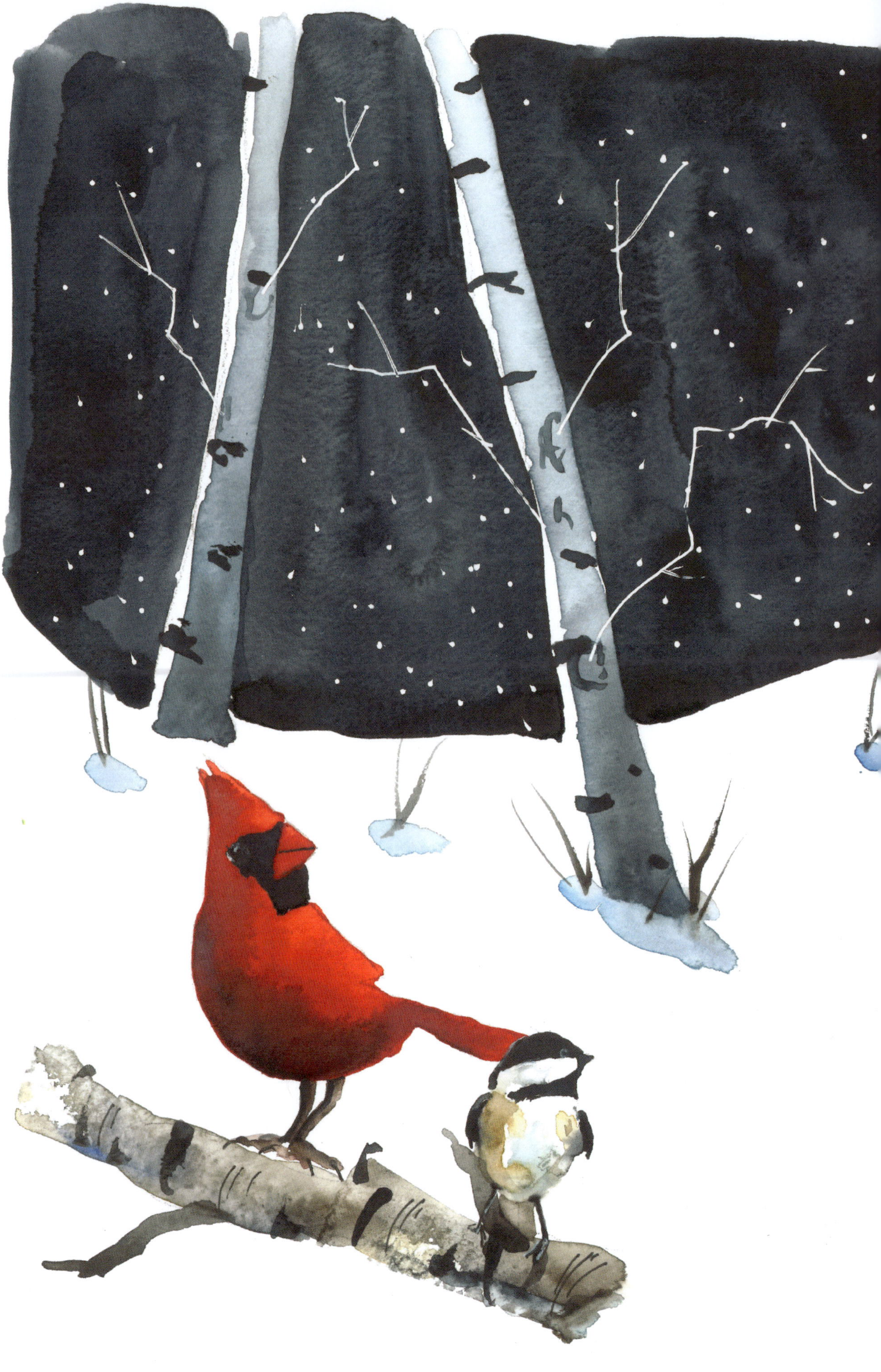

Rudy edged closer, then to his surprise,
the bird flapped its wings and opened its eyes.
"An owl, not me! I am a bat, don't you see?
An owl is a bird, not a mammal like me."

"I hoped for an owl so we could share a song.
Someday I'll meet one, and we'll sing all night long."

"Good luck with that," the bat said to the bird.
"The owl sings alone, that's all I ever heard."

One evening, a snowstorm kept Rudy tucked in tight
as he listened to hoots ring out all through the night.
The moon wasn't bright, just a glint in the sky,
but he followed the call for he knew he must try.

The wind howled and blasted, the sky filled with frost.
The hoots came less often; the trail soon got lost.

Rudy then heard the loud cawing of crows.
Noting their numbers, a plan soon arose.
The crows would know if an owl could be found.
Their very large crew flew in from all around.

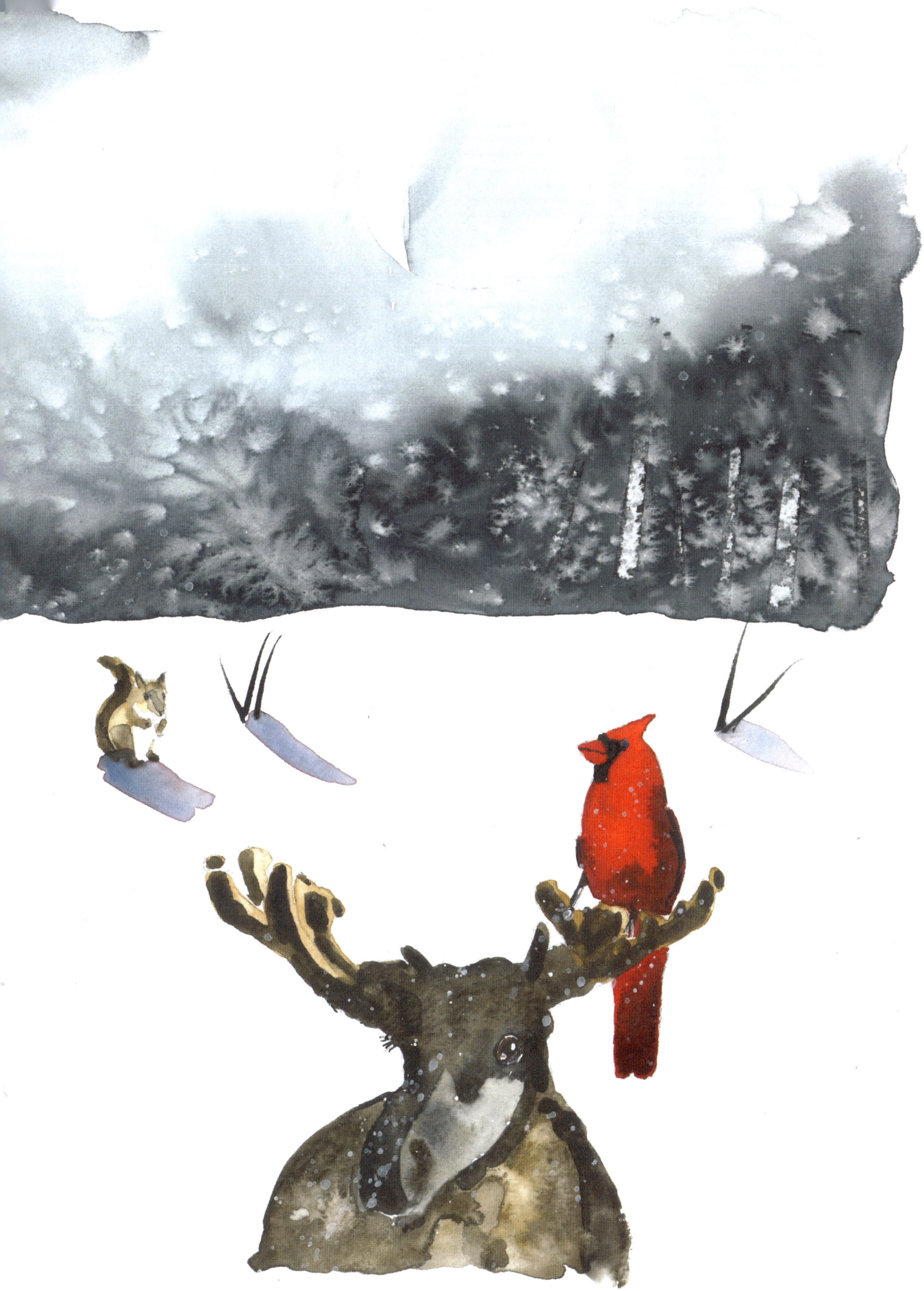

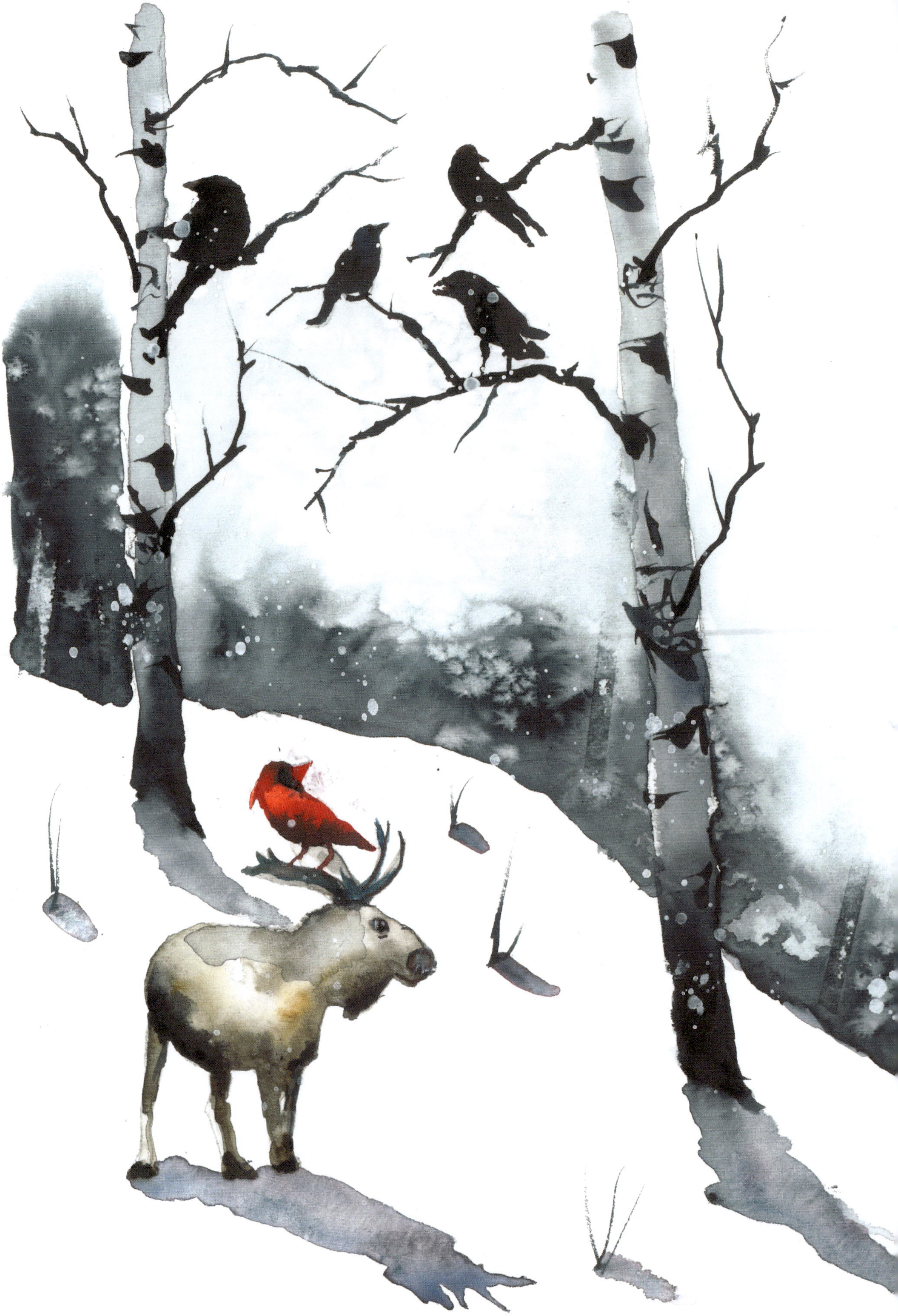

Once the group settled to roost for the night,
Rudy asked, "Has the owl been out tonight?"

They shook their heads, one by one, and then all.
Not one had seen the owl, nor heard his call.

At last, a full round moon blazed bright in the sky, and Rudy was patient, but ready to fly.

He watched and listened for the owl's sweet cry.
And then there it was— his favorite lullaby!

Off Rudy went with not a moment to spare.
He studied the tree tops, alert and aware.
Then, what he saw filled his heart with delight.
An owl was hooting right there in his sight!

But the owl's features caused Rudy to pause.
His beak was gigantic, and sharp like his claws.

The owl flicked its ears and let out a *hoo*,
and Rudy knew just what he needed to do.
He puffed out his chest, and he steadied his feet.
Then, softly, he let out his most gentle tweet.

The two birds continued to sing their duet,
while Rudy got as close as he wanted to get.
The full moon was strong enough for him to see
the treasure tucked neatly inside the owl's tree.

The heads of three owlets peeked out from their nest.
The owl was just doing what all moms do best.

Then, from a distance, another hoot rang out,
and Rudy sensed what the owl's call was about.
"Do you *hoo-hoo* to talk with friends at night,
or is your call a warning to stay out of sight?"

"Tonight, I called out for a friend and found you.
Before you go, let's sing another song or two."

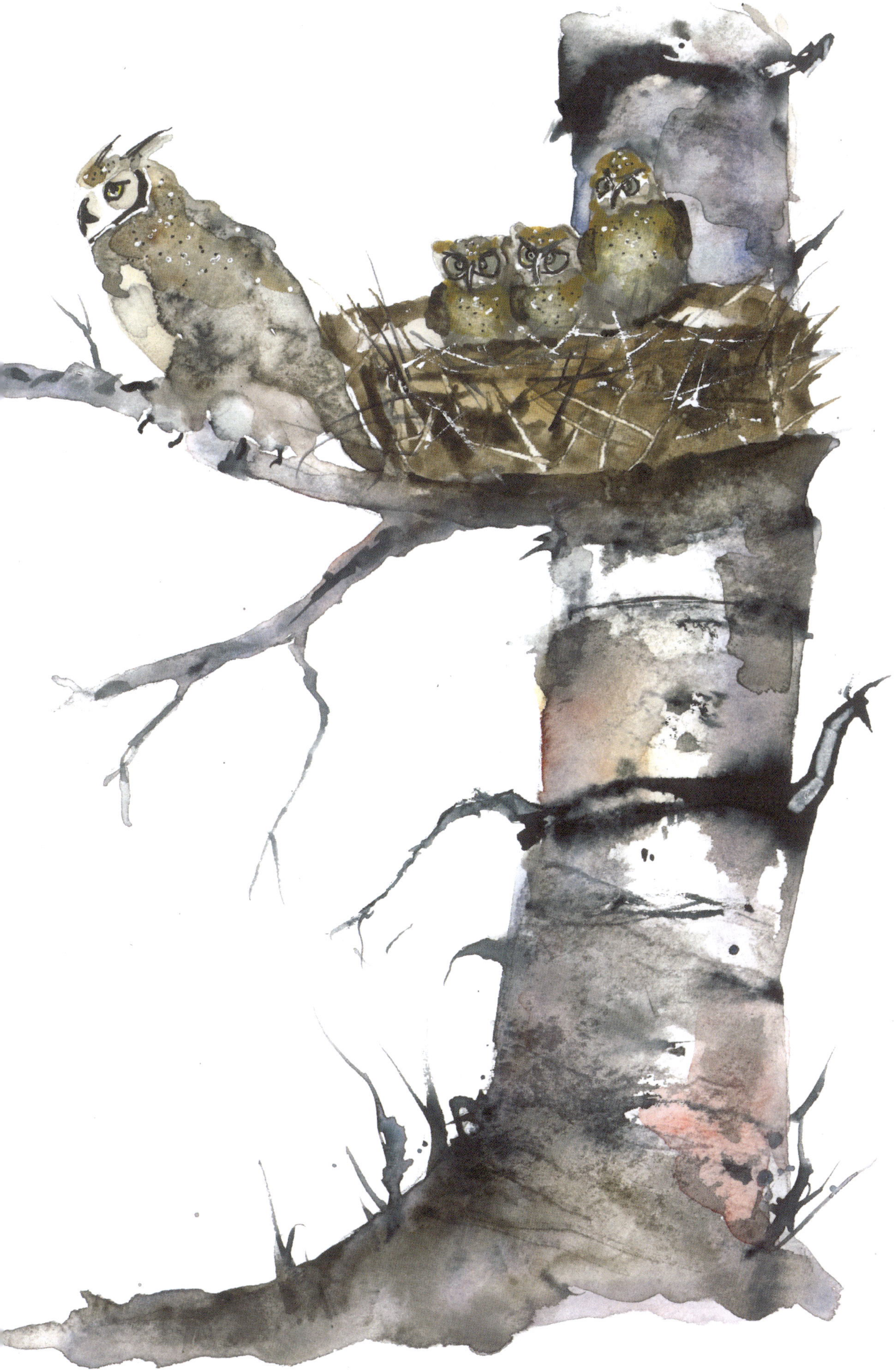

They chirped and *hoo-hooed* in patterns so new.
It was so much fun, they added some dancing too.

The moonlight was perfect for lighting the show.
Their concert together made everyone glow.

Back in his nest, his adventures behind,
Rudy recalled how the moon had been kind.

Feeling so blessed, he composed one more tune that carried his love all the way to the moon.

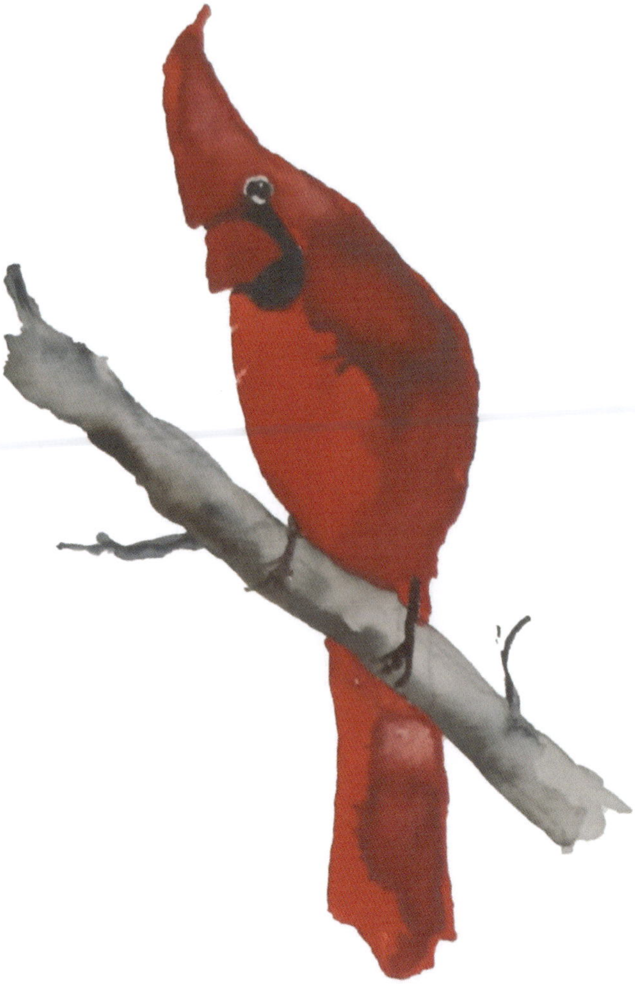

Dolores Frazer taught middle school for twenty years before she became a literacy specialist at the elementary level. *Rudy and the Owl* was inspired by her desire to help emerging readers experience the joy of storytelling while developing skills in reading and writing. More information about her works, including lesson plans for this story, can be found by visiting her author website at www.doloresfrazer.com.

Jim Lagasse is a watercolor artist from Bangor, Maine. His work has been published in regional and international magazines and has been featured in multiple television series and commercials, including *Blue Bloods*, *Saturday Night Live*, and HBO. Jim has been painting for over thirty years and continues to paint New England landscapes and children's book art. You can see a selection of his portfolio by visiting his artist website at www.pinetreeart.etsy.com.

Printed in Great Britain
by Amazon